THE FAMOUS FIVE
SHORT STORIES

GEORGE'S HAIR IS TOO LONG

The Famous Five

Timmy   Anne   Dick   Julian   George

Text first published in Great Britain in Enid Blyton's Magazine Annual – No. 2, in 1955.
Also available in The Famous Five Short Stories, published by Hodder Children's Books.
First published in Great Britain in this edition in 2014 by Hodder Children's Books

2

A Catalogue record for this book is available from the British Library
ISBN 978 1 444 91626 3

Hodder Children's Books
A division of Hachette Children's Books
Hachette UK Limited, 338 Euston Road, London NW1 3BH

www.hachette.co.uk

Enid Blyton

GEORGE'S HAIR IS TOO LONG

illustrated by **Jamie Littler**

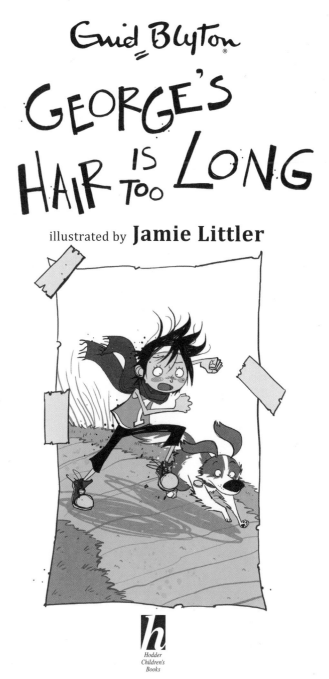

*Hodder
Children's
Books*

A division of Hachette Children's Books

Famous Five Colour Reads

Five and a Half-Term Adventure

George's Hair is Too Long

Good Old Timmy

A Lazy Afternoon

Well Done, Famous Five

Five Have a Puzzling Time

Happy Christmas, Five

When Timmy Chased the Cat

For a complete list of the full-length
Famous Five adventures, turn to
the last page of this book

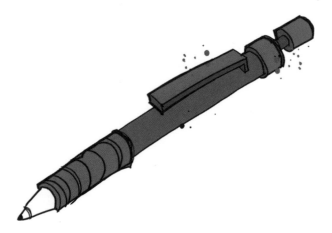

Contents

chapter 1   page 7

chapter 2   page 13

chapter 3   page 23

chapter 4   page 33

Chapter 5   page 43

chapter 6   page 55

chapter 7   page 63

Chapter 8   page 77

CHAPTER ONE

'Let's go to **Windy Cove**,' said
Julian one fine summer's day in August.
'It's so hot on Kirrin Beach – Windy Cove
will be nice and cool. There's always a breeze
blowing there.'

'Right,' said Dick. 'What do you say, George?'

'Well, I wanted to go and have my **hair cut,'** said George. **'Honestly, it'll be as long as Anne's if I don't have it cut soon.'**

'Well, I wish you *would* have it cut,' said Dick. 'You keep on complaining about it – as if it mattered whether it was short or long.'

'You forget that it matters to George very much,' said Julian with a grin. **'People might mistake her for a girl if it grows half an inch longer!** Well, for goodness' sake, George, get it **cut this afternoon**. We pass **the hairdresser's** on the way to Windy Cove. We'll all go into the dairy and have **ice-creams**, and wait for you there.'

They set off at two o'clock. The road to the village was hot and dusty, and Timmy ran along with his long pink tongue hanging halfway down his front legs!

'Poor Tim – you can have an ice-cream, too,' said Dick, patting him.

CHAPTER TWO.

They came to the village, and George went to the **hairdresser's shop** while the others went on with Timmy to the **dairy,** which sold good creamy ice-creams. They heard George calling them and turned.

'**The shop's shut! It's early-closing day,**' she shouted. 'I forgot. **Now I can't have my hair cut.**'

'**Well, never mind – come and have an ice-cream,**' shouted back Julian.

But George was in an obstinate mood. '**No. I want my hair cut, even if I have to cut it myself! Anybody got a pair of scissors?**'

'**Of course not.** Who carries scissors about? Don't be an idiot!' said Dick. 'For goodness' sake **come on with us** and **stop worrying about your hair.**'

'I'll go **and borrow** some **scissors** in the **ironmonger's,'** shouted George. **'They're shut, too,** but I know old Mr Pails will let me in at the **side door.** You go on with Timmy and have ice-creams. I don't want one. **I'll catch you up when I'm ready.'**

16

'What an idiot George is,' said Dick, going on with the others. 'Once she's made up her mind to do something, nothing will stop her, not even if it doesn't really matter.'

They went to the **dairy.** George went round to the **side door** of the **ironmonger's shop.**

Mr Pails answered her knock. 'Well, George, what do you want?' he said. **'My shop's shut,** as you very well know, and I'm just going to **catch the bus** over to my son's, **as I *always* do on early-closing day.'**

'I won't keep you more than a minute,' said George. 'I want to **borrow** a pair of **nice sharp scissors,** Mr Pails. Only just for **a minute or two.** The bus doesn't go for **ten minutes;** you've got plenty of time.'

'Well, well, you always were a one for getting your own way!' said the old man. 'Come on in – I'll show you the drawer where the scissors are kept. **But don't you be long now – I must catch that bus!'**

CHAPTER THREE

George went **down the passage** that led to the shop and the old man took her to a drawer **at the back.** He was just opening it when a **small van** drew up **outside the shop**.

23

It stopped and **two men** got out. George looked up casually – and **jumped!** One of the men was **peering** through the **letterbox** on the **shop door.** What an **extraordinary** thing to do!

George distinctly saw the **man's eyes** looking through the letterbox into the **dark shop**. She pulled at Mr Pails' arm and whispered. 'Do you see that man peering through the letterbox? **What does he want?** He couldn't have seen us because we're in such a dark corner.'

At that very moment the **door was forced open** and **two men came hurriedly into the shop.**

At first they didn't see Mr Pails and George,

and made for the **little black safe**

set at the back of the counter. Mr Pails gave

an indignant shout.

'**Hey, you! What do you mean, forcing your way in here? I'll …**'

But one of the men leapt over to him and put **his hand** over the **old man's mouth.** The other man ran to George and **swung her into a little cupboard** nearby, paying no attention to her yells.

Mr Pails was **shoved**
in, too, and the door was **forced shut**
on them and **locked.**

George **shouted** at the top of her **voice,** and so did Mr Pails. But the shop was set apart from the others in the street, and there was no one to hear them on that hot, stifling afternoon.

George heard the sound of panting as the **men removed the heavy little safe.** Then the **shop door shut,** and there was the sound of the van being started up – and **driven away!**

CHAPTER FOUR

'If only I'd had **Timmy** with me,' thought George fiercely, as she pushed hard against the door. 'Why did I say he could go and have an ice-cream with the others?'

Mr Pails was **almost fainting** with **shock and fright,** and was no help at all. George gave up struggling with the door after a while, and began to wish there weren't so many pans and brushes stored in the cupboard, leaving so little room for her and the old ironmonger!

34

She wondered what the others were doing. Would they come back and look for her? If they did, she could yell again.

But the others had now finished their ice-creams and were on the way to Windy Cove. George had said she didn't want an ice-cream, but would catch them up. Very well, they would walk on and she could overtake them.

So off they went along the road that led to **Windy Cove,** Timmy lagging behind a little on the lookout for **his beloved George.** *Why didn't she come?*

He suddenly decided to **go back and look** for her. He felt anxious, although he didn't know why. He turned tail and trotted off back to the village.

'There goes Tim,' said Anne with a laugh. 'He can't bear to be without **George** for more than half an hour! **Goodbye, Tim! Tell George** to **hurry up!'**

They went on their way without Timmy, walking in a line across a narrow lane.

37

Suddenly a van turned a corner behind them and came racing up at top speed. **Dick only just dragged Anne** out of its way in time. The van **swerved** and went on, **hooting wildly** at the next corner.

'What does **the driver think he's doing?'** said Dick angrily. **'Tearing** down narrow, winding lanes like that! **What's his hurry?'**

The van turned the corner – and almost immediately after there came an **explosive noise** and the **scream** of brakes. Then a silence.

CHAPTER FIVE

'**Whew! That sounded like a burst tyre,**' said Julian, beginning to run. 'I hope they haven't had **an accident.**'

The three turned the corner. They saw the van slewed round in the lane, almost in the ditch. The tyre on the left-hand back wheel was **flat** and had **split badly.** It certainly was a **very burst tyre** indeed! **Two men** were looking at it **angrily.**

44

'**Here, you!**' said one of the men, turning to Dick. 'Run to the **nearest garage, will you, and ask a man to come and help us?'**

'**Definitely not!**' said Dick. '**You nearly knocked over my sister** just now. One of you can go and get help yourselves. You'd no right to drive along a country lane like that.'

But neither of the men made a move to go back for help. Instead, **they scowled at the burst tyre and at each other.** The three stood there, looking with interest at the angry men.

'**You clear off,**' said one of the men at last. '**Unless you want to help us with the wheel.** Do you know how to change a wheel?'

'**Yes,**' said Julian, sitting down on the hedge bank. 'Don't you? It's funny if you don't know. **As your job is driving a van,** I'd have thought it'd be one of **the first things you'd learn!**'

'**You shut up,**' said the first man, '**and clear off.**'

'**Why?**' said Dick, sitting down beside Julian. 'You seem **very keen to get rid of us,** don't you? Or do you feel nervous that experts like us should watch you making a mess of such a simple thing as changing a wheel?'

48

Anne didn't like all this. 'I think I'll go back and meet George,' she said, and walked round the van. She took a quick look inside – and **saw a little black safe there!**

A safe! She took a quick glance back at the two men. They certainly were a **nasty-looking couple.** She went over to Julian and sat down beside him. She took **a twig and began to write** idly **in the thick dust at their feet, nudging him** as she did so.

Julian **looked down** into the dust at once.

'A safe is in the van,'

Anne had **written in the dust,** and, as soon as she knew that the boys had seen what she had written, she **rubbed her foot over** the hurried writing.

The three stared at the two men, who were now trying to change the wheel. It was obvious that they had **never changed one before!** Julian caught hold of Anne when she got up to go back and meet George.

'**No. Stay,**' he said. 'George may have changed her mind and gone home. **You stay with us, Anne.**'

So Anne stayed, hoping against hope that George would soon appear with Timmy. **Why was she so long?** She must have **gone home, after all!** What was Julian going to do? Wait for another car to come along, and then stop it and pass on his suspicions to the driver? Because the whole thing was **very suspicious!** Anne was certain that both safe and van were stolen.

Where was George? She had had plenty of time to borrow scissors, cut her hair **and catch them up!**

CHAPTER SIX

Poor George had stood in the cupboard till she was so cramped that she could hardly move an arm or leg. Mr Pails seemed to have fainted, but she couldn't do anything about it. And then she heard a **very familiar and welcome sound!**

Feet pattered down the passage that led to the back of the shop, and then came **a whine. Timmy!**

'Timmy! Tim, I'm here, in this cupboard!' called George. **'Timmy!'**

Timmy came and **scraped** at the cupboard, and then began **to bark so furiously** that **a passer-by stopped in surprise.** He pushed at the door, which had been left unlocked by the two thieves, and looked inside. **He saw Timmy at once. The dog ran to him and then back to the cupboard,** still barking.

'**Anyone here?**' called the passer-by.

'**Yes, yes – we're locked in this cupboard!**' cried George. '**Let us out, please.**'

It took only two seconds for the man to run across the floor and **unlock the cupboard.**

George staggered out, and Timmy flung himself on her, **licking her from head to foot.** Mr Pails was then **dragged out,** but he was so shocked and upset that it was difficult to get anything out of him.

'**Police!**' he kept saying. '**Police!**'

'I'll send someone for **the police – and a doctor, too,**' said the man. 'You sit down in that chair, Mr Pails. **I'll look after you.**'

George slipped out of the shop. She felt rather faint after her long stay in the cramped cupboard.

She must **hurry** **after the others**, tell them what had happened, and get them **to come back to the shop.** It was no use going to **Windy Cove that afternoon!**

CHAPTER SEVEN

So she and Timmy hurried down the dusty lane that led from the village to Windy Cove. How far had the others got? Perhaps they were at the cove now!

But they weren't. They were still sitting at the side of the lane, watching two perspiring, harassed, fumbling men trying to put on **a second wheel** after having spent ages **getting the first one off!**

There weren't enough
tools to do the job properly, as Julian
could very well see. He wished George
would come. **Timmy would be such a help!**

And then, **round the corner came George at last, with Timmy at her heels.** Rather a pale George, evidently bursting with news. She raced up to them.

'Guess what happened to me? Mr Pails and I were **locked in a cupboard in his shop by two thieves** who…'

She suddenly caught sight of the
two men tinkering with the van,
and stopped, astounded.

She pointed at them and shouted.

'Those are the two men! And that's the van they came in – have they got a safe in it?'

'Yes,' said Julian, standing up very suddenly. **'They have!** Are you sure you recognize these men, George?'

'Oh yes! I'll never forget them all my life!' cried George. **'Timmy – watch them! Watch them, Timmy!'**

Timmy sprang over to the two men, **growling so fiercely** and showing all his white teeth in such a snarl that **the two men shrank back, terrified.** One raised a hand as if to strike Timmy with the tool he held.

'If you hit him, he'll have you down on the ground at once,' warned George grimly, and the man dropped his hand. 'Now – what do we do, Julian? These men ought to be handed over to the police.'

'Listen –
here comes
a car,' said Dick.
'We can **stop it** and
send **a message** back to the village.'

A big car came round the corner from
the direction of Windy Cove. Julian **waved
to it to stop**. Two men were in it.

'What's up?' they called.

Julian explained as shortly as he could.

One of the men jumped down immediately. **'You want the police at once,'** he said. **'Let's put that wheel on, and take the two men back to Kirrin Village**. My friend can drive the van, and **the boy** with the dog can go in the van with them! You others can get into my car, and we'll **follow the van** back to **Kirrin** and **get the police!'**

This all sounded very sane and sensible.

The **wheel was put on** in a flash, the two men bundled into the back of the van with a **snarling Timmy,** and **George (pleased because she had been mistaken for a boy!)** sat in the front of the van with the man from the other car.

They drove off, followed by the big car, in which were a pleased and smiling **Julian, Dick and Anne!**

CHAPTER EIGHT

It was **very exciting** when they all got to **Kirrin Village!** The police were amazed and delighted to have the **two robbers** safely delivered to them, with **the safe** and the **stolen van as well!**

Mr Pails was **very, very grateful.** Timmy was half sorry he hadn't been allowed even a **small bite, but extremely happy** to **have been able to rescue** his **beloved George!**

'**Well – what a thrill!**' said George's mother, when they arrived home at last and told their astonishing tale. 'So you **didn't get to Windy Cove, after all.** Still – **you can all go tomorrow!**'

'**I can't,**' said George at once.

'**WHY?**' asked everyone, surprised.

'**Because – I absolutely – must – get – my – hair – cut!**' said George. 'And I'll make sure **I'm not** locked in a cupboard next time!'